Looking at
Bugs

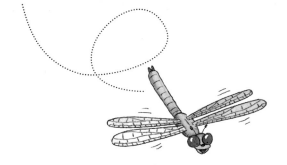

Library of Congress Cataloging-in-Publication Data

Driscoll, Laura.

Looking at bugs / by Laura Driscoll; illustrated by Deborah Drew-Brook-Cormack, Allan Drew-Brook-Cormack, and Tim Haggerty.

p. cm. - (My first field guides)

ISBN 0-448-42487-8

1. Insects-Juvenile literature. [1. Insects.] I. Drew-Brook-Cormack, Deborah, ill. II. Drew-Brook-Cormack, Allan, ill. III. Haggerty, Tim, ill. IV. Title. V. Series.

QL 467.2 .D75 2001

595.7-dc21   2001033358

photo credits: cover and p.3 (butterfly) © TSM/Bob London, 1998; p.6 ANIMALS ANIMALS © Donald Specker; p.7 © 1998 Larry Barns c/o Mira; p.16 ANIMALS ANIMALS © Robert Lubeck; p.20 ANIMALS ANIMALS © Patti Murray; p.25 (orb web) ANIMALS ANIMALS © E. R. Degginger, (funnel web) ANIMALS ANIMALS © Donald Specker, (house spider web) ANIMALS ANIMALS © Zig Leszczynski; p.33 © George Lepp/CORBIS, © TSM/Gavriel Jecan, 1998, © 1995 Ralph G. Krubner c/o Mira; p.39 ANIMALS ANIMALS © John Pontier; p.41 ANIMALS ANIMALS © Zig Leszczynski.

ISBN 0-448-42487-8   A B C D E F G H I J

MY FIRST FIELD GUIDE

Looking at Bugs

By Laura Driscoll

Illustrated by
Deborah and Allan Drew-Brook-Cormack
and Tim Haggerty

Grosset & Dunlap • New York

What Makes a Bug a Bug?

Bugs are everywhere.
They have been on Earth
a lot longer than we have.
Even before the dinosaurs,
there were bugs.
What exactly makes a bug
a bug?

Insect Checklist

All adult insects have:

1. A body with 3 parts: head, thorax, abdomen
2. 6 legs
3. A hard outer skeleton that is like armor

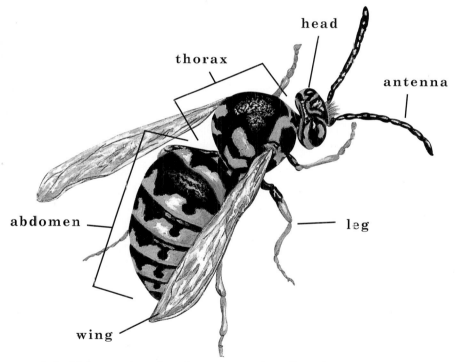

Adult insects also have a pair of antennas. They may have other things, too, like wings. But to be a bug, it has to have the 3 things on the list.

Growing Up

newly hatched true bugs
and their egg shells

Insects begin their lives as eggs.
When they hatch, some look like tiny
copies of their parents. As the little
insect grows, it gets too big for its outer
skeleton. So it sheds and grows a new
one. Grasshoppers grow this way.

Other baby insects don't look at all like their parents. When a butterfly egg hatches, a caterpillar crawls out.
It looks more like a worm than a bug.
But then it changes. A caterpillar wraps itself up in a sack. Inside, the caterpillar turns into a butterfly with wings.
It breaks open the sack and flies away.

There are more than 1 million kinds of insects. The stick insect is the longest. It is almost 2 feet long!

Bug Hunting

You may want to pick up some of the insects you find. But that's not a good idea unless you are sure that the bug doesn't sting or bite. Also, you might hurt the bug. So it's better just to look.

A park or even a puddle can be a great place to find bugs. Check under leaves and rocks and on tree trunks. But be gentle. Try to leave things the way you found them. Be careful and quiet. You will see more bugs that way.

Calling All Bugs!

Try to get bugs to come to you.

 Put an apple core on the ground.

Come back in a few hours.

 See who has come for a snack.

Later, ask an adult to check the apple for any stinging bugs.

 Then put it in the trash.

Be Careful

Wear long pants and long sleeves even in spring or summer. This will help protect you from poison ivy and tick bites.

poison ivy

ticks

Check me out, mom!

Always check yourself after bug hunting. (Have someone else check the places you can't see.)

When to Look

You will find more bugs during warm months. In the winter, many come inside to keep warm. They find hiding places and sleep.

During the winter, go on an indoor bug hunt. Check in corners and in stacks of newspapers. Look around plants, and in firewood piles. Chances are you will find some insects.

How to Use This Book

The insects in this book are very common. See if you can find them all! When you find one, take the sticker of that insect from the sticker page.

Stick it in the space on that bug's page. Write down where and when you found it in the Field Notes in the back of the book.

Remember: there are many different kinds of the same bug. For example, there are at least 150,000 kinds of moths. You may find a different moth from the moths in this book. That's okay—it still counts! Try drawing any bug you don't know on one of the Field Notes pages. Maybe a teacher or another grown-up can help you figure out what bug you saw.

Ants

Ants are skinny
and have a
tiny waist.
Their feelers
are jointed.
Some ants
have wings.
Some don't.

red ant

Where to Look

Check in backyards or parks.

Size

$1/16$" to 1"

Careful!

Don't disturb an anthill. Almost
all ants can sting or bite if you bother them.

winged
harvester
ant

Ants live together in nests underground or inside dead wood. A group of ants is called a colony. Each colony has a queen. She lays all of the eggs. The other ants are the workers. The workers find food for the colony. They also protect the queen.

I found an
ant

place your
sticker here

Ants are very strong for their size.
Some ants carry things
fifty times heavier than they are.
That's like your mom carrying a car!

The Great Taste Test

Ants like sweet foods.
But do they like some kinds of sweets
more than others?

Put two
packets of
sugar in one
cup of water.

Put two
packets of
sweetener in
the other cup.

Stir the cups with a different spoon.
Now find an anthill.

Pour one
cup a few
feet from
the anthill.

Pour the
other cup
on the
other side.

Come back in 2 hours.
Which spot has more ants? Check to see if any
other bugs have found the sweet spots.

Bees

What to Look For

Bees are black or brown with white, yellow, or orange bands. They have 2 short back wings and 2 longer front wings. Their round bodies are covered with feathery hairs.

Where to Look

Around flowers in gardens, fields, and open woods.

Size

⅛" to 1"

Honeybees make honey. They store it in their hives.

Honeybees and bumblebees
are the most well-known bees.
Like ants, they live together
in colonies with a queen.

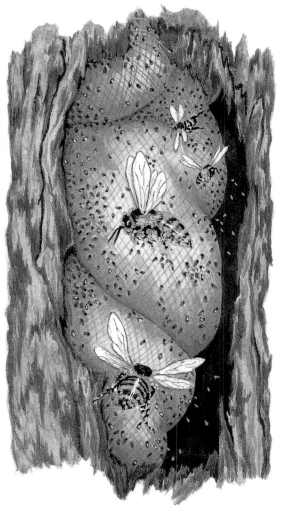

Most bees
can sting. But
they usually
do only to
defend their
nest or hive.
So stay clear
of beehives!

I found a
bee

place your
sticker here

Bees eat flower nectar.
As they take the nectar from the flower,
flower pollen sticks to bees.
Then, when the bees visit other flowers,
some of the pollen falls off.
This helps make new flowers.
If it weren't for bees, there wouldn't
be so many flowers on Earth!

Wasps

What to Look For
Wasps look like bees. But they are not as round and they are not hairy. They are usually black and yellow, or black and white.

Where to Look
Wasps live in nests, but you can often find them near garbage cans in parks.

Size
about ½"

Careful!
Some wasps can be very quick to sting.

I found a
wasp

place your
sticker here

Flies

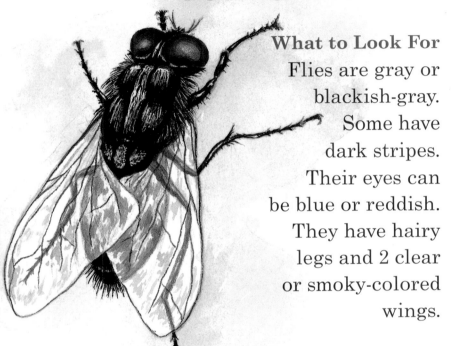

What to Look For
Flies are gray or blackish-gray. Some have dark stripes. Their eyes can be blue or reddish. They have hairy legs and 2 clear or smoky-colored wings.

Where to Look
Swamps, marshes, ponds, near running water in woods, and near garbage cans and rotting food.

Size
¹/₄" to ¹/₂"

How do flies walk on ceilings?
How do they walk up mirrors,
windows, and other slippery places?
Flies have tiny claws
and sticky pads on their feet.
This helps them keep their hold.

Some female
flies can lay up
to 720 eggs!
No wonder there
are so many
of these
pesky insects.

I found a
fly

place your
sticker here

Spiders

What to Look For

Most spiders are black, brown, or gray. They usually have round bodies with long thin legs. Spiders have 8 legs and only 2 body parts. So are they bugs? No! Spiders do <u>not</u> pass the insect test. But people think of spiders as bugs. That's why they are in this book.

Where to Look

In fields, on tree trunks, and on the ground.

Size

$\frac{1}{4}$" to 1 $\frac{1}{2}$"

Some people think of spiders as "good bugs." That's because they eat lots of insect pests; insects that get caught in their webs make a tasty meal for spiders!

Whose Web is This?

Different kinds of spiders spin different webs.

Orb-weaving spiders make the most beautiful webs.

Outdoors, funnel web spiders spin webs in the grass and bushes.

House spiders make tangled and messy webs.

I found a
spider

place your
sticker here.

Beetles

What to Look For

Beetles come in lots
of colors: brown,
black, red, yellow,
blue, green—
you name it!
Some have
dark spots
or other marks.
Many beetles
are round
and shiny.
They have 2 front wings and
2 back wings that fold.

Where to Look

Forests, fields and other grassy
areas, under rocks and logs.

Size

⅛" to 1"

**common black
ground beetle**

Most beetles are small. But the Goliath beetle is 4 ½ inches long and weighs up to 3 ½ ounces. That's as much as a hamburger!

There are more than 350,000 kinds of beetles on Earth! Some have bright colors that protect them. The colors let other animals know that beetles taste bad. So the animals don't eat them.

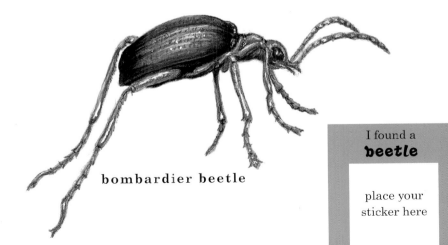

bombardier beetle

I found a
beetle

place your
sticker here

Ladybugs

What to Look For

Ladybugs are a type of beetle. These oval-shaped bugs are small and shiny and have feelers and short legs. Their wings are often orange-red and have black spots.

Where to Look

Meadows, fields, woods, gardens, and sometimes inside homes.

Size

$1/8$" to $3/8$"

ash gray ladybug

nine-spot yellow ladybug

The ladybug is one of the most beloved
insects in the world. Why?
Well, for one thing, ladybugs are pretty.
But like spiders, they are also "good
bugs." They eat insects that are bad for
plants. Many gardeners buy ladybugs
and set them free in their gardens.

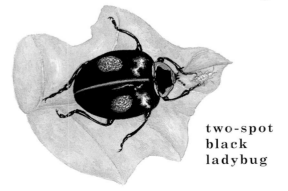

**two-spot
black
ladybug**

I found a
ladybug

place your
sticker here

Fireflies

What to Look For
These bugs have soft, flat bodies and 2 feelers. They are usually brown. They have 1 pair of wings that folds up on their backs. Last but not least, fireflies flash!

Where to Look
Look in tall grass and around ponds and streams.

When to Look
Look on cloudy evenings: fireflies blink the most when the moon is not out.

Size
¼" to ½"

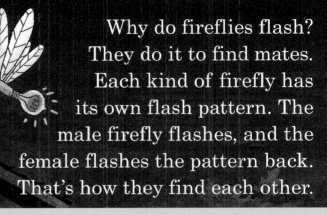

Why do fireflies flash?
They do it to find mates.
Each kind of firefly has
its own flash pattern. The
male firefly flashes, and the
female flashes the pattern back.
That's how they find each other.

Be a Firefly!

You can pretend to be a firefly.
You'll need a penlight.
Move away from house lights
and streetlights.
When you see a firefly flash,
look at its flash pattern.
Then flash the same
pattern with your light.

I found a
firefly

place your
sticker here

If you do it right,
the firefly may fly over!

Butterflies

What to Look For

Butterflies have 4 large wings with small scales on them. On many butterflies, the scales are brightly colored. The body is long and thin, and usually dark-colored.

Where to Look

Look around low plants, gardens, or at the butterfly house at the zoo.

When to Look

During warmer months (May to August).

Size

Wings spread from $\frac{1}{4}$" to 4".

There are more than 12,000 kinds of butterflies. Butterflies come in lots of colors. The bright colors help butterflies find mates of their own kind. Some bright colors also tell other animals that butterflies taste bad. So the animals leave the butterflies alone and look for a better snack!

tailed jay butterfly

western tiger swallowtail butterfly

heliconius ismenius butterfly

I found a
butterfly

place your sticker here

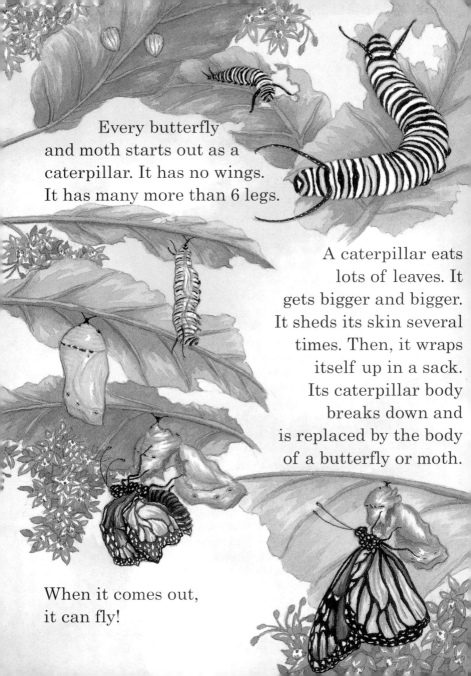

Every butterfly and moth starts out as a caterpillar. It has no wings. It has many more than 6 legs.

A caterpillar eats lots of leaves. It gets bigger and bigger. It sheds its skin several times. Then, it wraps itself up in a sack. Its caterpillar body breaks down and is replaced by the body of a butterfly or moth.

When it comes out, it can fly!

Butterflies eat
flower nectar.
They use their
long tongues to
sip the nectar—
like sipping through
a straw.

Butterflies are never
out in rain. Rain can
hurt their wings.

Moths

What to Look For
Like butterflies, moths have 4 large wings with small scales. The scales can be colored, but most moths do not have bright wings like butterflies. They are usually light brown or gray. Some have lighter or darker markings.

Where to Look
In woods, or turn on your porch light.
(Moths fly to white light – not yellow.)

When to Look
Evenings from May to August.

Size
Wings spread from $\frac{1}{4}$" to 1 $\frac{1}{2}$"

There are two big differences between butterflies and moths.

Butterflies fly during the day.

Moths fly at night.

And most butterflies have bright colors.
Most moths are brown or gray.
Moths can blend in with their surroundings. This helps them hide from birds and other enemies.

I found a
moth

place your
sticker here

Grasshoppers

What to Look For
Grasshoppers can be pale green, brown, or brownish yellow. Most of them have 2 large back wings and 2 narrow front wings. They have very long back legs that are bent. Their "knees" stick up in the air.

Where to Look
Fields, meadows, and open woods.
Check in places with lots of leaves for them to eat.

Size
1" to 4"

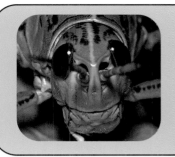

After you find a grasshopper, look for its 5 eyes. It has 1 on either side of its head and 3 more on top!

Grasshoppers are great jumpers. A grasshopper can jump 20 times the length of its body. (That's like you jumping over two buses!)

When a grasshopper gets scared, it usually just jumps away. But it may also spit some brown liquid. Scientists think the spit protects them against other bugs.

I found a
grasshopper

place your
sticker here

Crickets

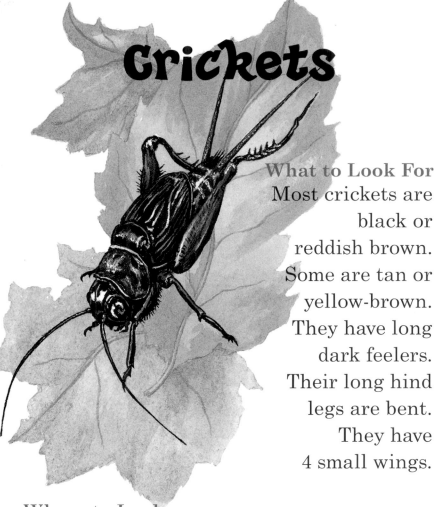

What to Look For

Most crickets are black or reddish brown. Some are tan or yellow-brown. They have long dark feelers. Their long hind legs are bent. They have 4 small wings.

Where to Look

In lawns, fields, and woods where it is not windy.

When to Look

Crickets hide during the day. Look for them after dark.

Size

about 1"

house cricket

Some crickets like light. So grab your flashlight and follow the chirping! When you get close, put your flashlight down in the grass. You should get one or two cricket visitors.

Crickets are known for their chirping. But only male crickets chirp. How? By rubbing their two front wings together. They are calling to female crickets!

I found a
cricket

place your
sticker here

Cockroaches

What to Look For
These are shiny, light or dark brown bugs. Their thin antennae are longer than their bodies. Cockroaches look a little bit like crickets, but their back legs are not as long. They have 4 wings that fold up.

Where to Look
In cracks in warm, damp places inside buildings.

Size
Size: ½" to 2"

Most people hate cockroaches. Usually they are found inside homes and apartments. Roaches can eat almost anything: glue, paper, soap, plus human and pet food.

But not everyone hates cockroaches. The Madagascar hissing cockroach is a popular class pet in some schools. These big roaches are clean and do not smell.

I found a
cockroach

place your
sticker here

Mosquitoes

What to Look For
These bugs are light brown or brownish-gray, with 2 wings and long thin legs. Their long thin mouthparts can suck blood from mammals.

Where to Look
Swamps, ponds, and other areas of standing water.

Size
about 1/4"

A mosquito can smell a person 90 feet away!

Mosquitoes are the bugs of summer. On warm evenings, they will be looking for you. Try to stay away!

Mosquitoes can carry germs that make people sick. Most mosquitoes come out at sunrise and at sunset. That's when people get bitten the most. (Only the females bite.) The female sticks its long mouthpart into a person's skin. Then it sucks up the blood.

I found a
mosquito

place your
sticker here.

Dragonflies

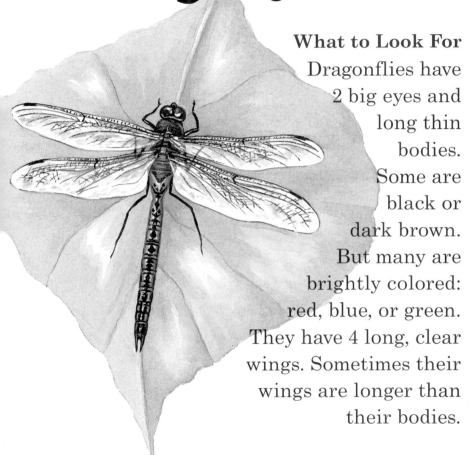

What to Look For
Dragonflies have 2 big eyes and long thin bodies. Some are black or dark brown. But many are brightly colored: red, blue, or green. They have 4 long, clear wings. Sometimes their wings are longer than their bodies.

Where to Look
Near streams, ponds, and in marshy areas.

Size
$^3/_4$" to 3"

Dragonflies are expert flyers. They can zip this way and that. They can even hover in mid-air like a helicopter.

Dragonfly eggs hatch in the water.
A baby dragonfly does not have wings.
It swims just under the water.
Then, at a certain time, it crawls out of the water. It sits on a rock or tree branch. It sheds its skin and becomes an adult—with long, clear wings. Then it takes off and starts doing stunts!

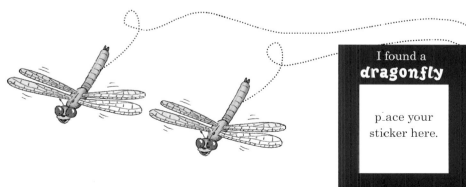

I found a
dragonfly

place your
sticker here.

Water Striders

What to Look For

These are dark brown or black insects with long thin legs. The 2 front legs are much shorter than the 4 back legs. The body looks flat. Most water striders do not have wings.

Where to Look

Look for "dimples" on the top of ponds and slow streams.

Size

about $1/2$"

I found a
water strider

place your
sticker here

Looking At
Bugs

My Field Notes

*Use these pages
 to write down or
 draw what you
 see when you are
 bug hunting.

Be a Bug's Shadow

Follow an insect around-bugs are
fascinating to watch! Use these pages
to write down what you see.

Bug Homes

Write down where bugs live . . .

...or draw it!

Bug Food

Write down what bugs eat . . .

...or draw it!

Busy Bugs

Write down what you see
bugs doing . . .

...or draw it!

Mystery Bugs

If you see a bug and can't tell from
this book what kind it is, draw the
bug's picture. Maybe later you will
see one in another book.

Color:

Size:

Where I saw it:

My Notes:

It looks like this:

Mystery Bugs

Color:

Size:

Where I saw it:

My Notes:

It looks like this:

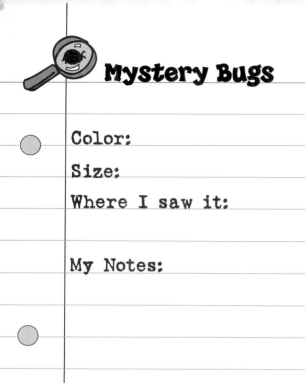

Mystery Bugs

Color:

Size:

Where I saw it:

My Notes:

It looks like this:

Mystery Bugs

Color:

Size:

Where I saw it:

My Notes:

It looks like this:

More Notes: